My FAVORITE FAIRY TALES

This book belongs to

_____

Age _____

Contents

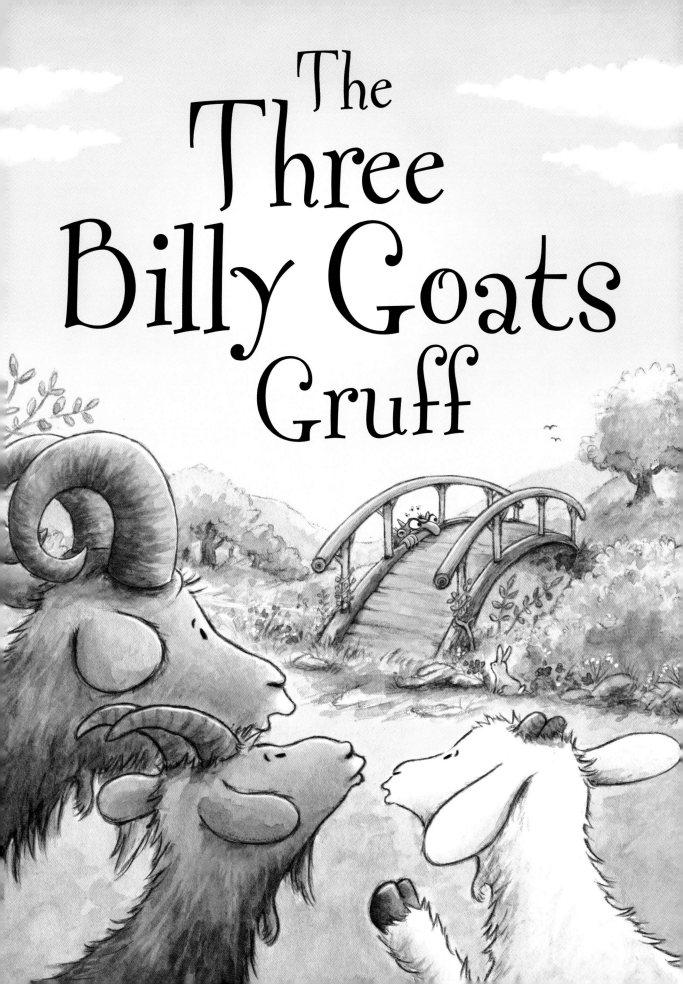

The Three Billy Goats Gruff

Once upon a time there were three billy goats. They were all called Gruff.

One day, the three Billy Goats Gruff set off to look for some fresh grass to eat.

In a meadow on the other side of a river,
they saw the best, greenest grass ever.

But to get to the grass they had to cross
a bridge over the river.

No one dared to cross the bridge because a **terrible troll** lived under it!

Then the three Billy Goats Gruff had an idea.
The little Billy Goat Gruff would go first.

Nervously, he stepped onto the bridge.

Trit-trot, trit-trot, he went.

"Who's that trit-trotting over my bridge?" shouted the *terrible troll*.

"I'm the little Billy Goat Gruff," said the goat. "I'm a *troll*, fol-de-rol, and I'll eat you for my supper!" bellowed the *terrible troll*.

"Please don't eat me. I'm too skinny to eat," said the little Billy Goat Gruff.

"My brother will be here soon. He's bigger than me and much tastier."

The *terrible troll* was greedy, so he decided to wait for the bigger, tastier goat.

He allowed the little Billy Goat Gruff to cross the bridge into the meadow where the best and greenest grass grew.

Next, it was the turn of the middle Billy Goat Gruff. He went slowly trit-trot, trit-trot over the bridge.

"Who's that trit-trotting over my bridge?" shouted the *terrible troll*.

"I'm the middle Billy Goat Gruff," said the goat.

"I'm a *troll*, fol-de-rol, and I'll eat you for my supper!" bellowed the *terrible troll*.

"Please don't eat me. I'm too skinny to eat," said the middle Billy Goat Gruff.
"My brother will be here soon.
He's **bigger** than me and much tastier."

17

Again, the *terrible troll* decided to wait for the **bigger**, tastier goat.

So he allowed the **middle Billy Goat Gruff** to cross the bridge into the meadow where the best and greenest grass grew.

Then it was the turn of the **big** Billy Goat Gruff.

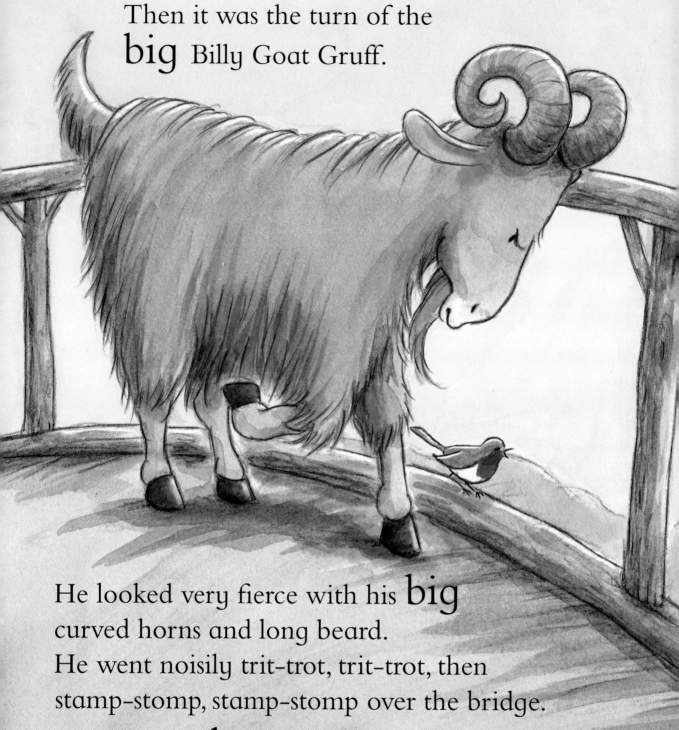

He looked very fierce with his **big** curved horns and long beard.
He went noisily trit-trot, trit-trot, then stamp-stomp, stamp-stomp over the bridge.

"Who's that trit-trotting over my bridge?" shouted the *terrible troll*.

"I'm the big Billy Goat Gruff!"

he shouted, louder than the *terrible troll!*

"I'm a **troll**, fol-de-rol, and I'll eat you for my supper!" bellowed the **terrible troll**.

"No you will not!"
BOOMED the big Billy Goat Gruff.
He stamped his hooves on the bridge,

STAMP-
STOMP

and then he bent his head low and
CHARGED!

The **big** Billy Goat Gruff butted the *terrible troll* with his **big** horns and knocked him straight off the bridge.

The **terrible troll** fell with a huge

splash!

into the
river below.

25

With the *terrible troll* gone, the **big** Billy Goat Gruff joined his brothers in the meadow where the best and greenest grass grew.

And no one saw the *terrible troll*

ever again!

Now everyone could cross the bridge in safety, and they all lived happily ever after.

Who's who?

Based on what they are saying, can you guess which character from the story each speech bubble belongs to?

"I was first into the meadow where the best and greenest grass grew. Who am I?"

"We sat on a rock in the greenest meadow after the *terrible troll* had gone. Who are we?"

"I butted the *terrible troll* into the river. Who am I?"

"I lived under the bridge. Who am I?"

"I am a goat with brown fur. Who am I?"

"I have a red tummy and flapped around by the bridge. Who am I?"

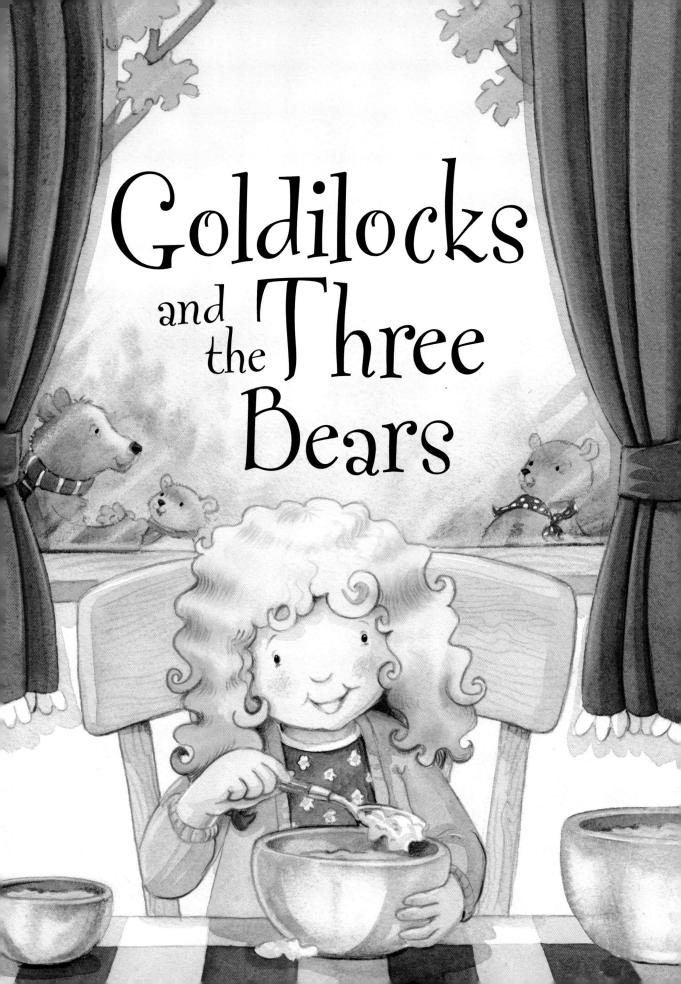

Goldilocks
and the Three Bears

Once upon a time there were three bears –
daddy bear, mommy bear, and baby bear.

One morning, mommy bear made some
porridge for breakfast.

She poured it into three bowls – a **big** bowl, a **middle**-sized bowl, and a little bowl.

The porridge was too hot to eat, so the three bears decided to go for a walk while it cooled down.

Goldilocks was also out walking in the forest that same morning. She spotted the three bears' cottage.

She knocked on the door, but no one replied.

She looked through the window. She could see that no one was at home, so she went inside.

Goldilocks was a very nosy little girl!

When Goldilocks saw the porridge on the table, she felt hungry.

She tasted the porridge in the biggest bowl – but it was too hot.

Next, she tasted the porridge in the middle-sized bowl – but it was too cold.

Then she tasted the porridge in the little bowl. It was just right – so she ate it all up!

When she had finished the porridge, Goldilocks saw three chairs in front of the fireplace.

She sat in the **biggest** chair – but it was too high.

Next, she sat in the middle-sized chair – but it was too low.

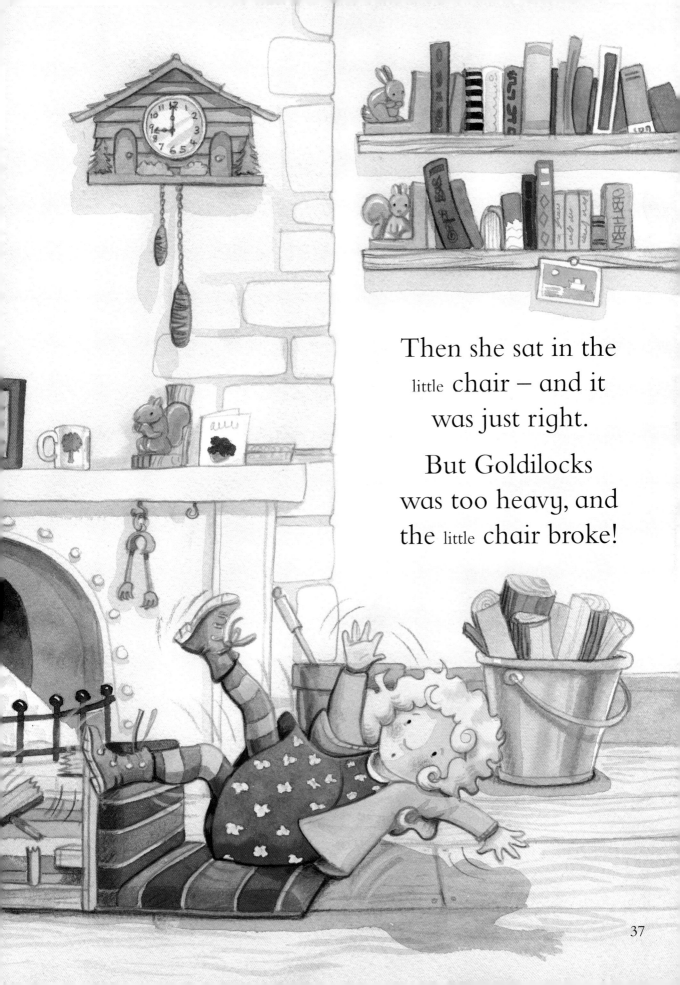

Then she sat in the little chair – and it was just right.

But Goldilocks was too heavy, and the little chair broke!

Now Goldilocks was feeling tired, so she climbed the stairs up to the bedroom.

She lay down on the
biggest bed –
but it was too hard.

Next, she tried the middle-sized bed – but it was too soft.

Then she tried the littlest bed – and it was just right. Goldilocks snuggled under the covers and was soon fast asleep!

Downstairs, the three
bears had returned home.
They knew immediately that
someone had been in their cottage.

"I'm sure I closed the door!"

said daddy bear.

The three bears saw the porridge
bowls on the table.

"Someone's been eating
my porridge!"
said daddy
bear in a big
booming voice.

"Someone's been eating
my porridge!"
said mommy bear in a
middle-sized voice.

"Someone's been eating my porridge!"

cried baby bear in a
squeaky little voice,

"and they've eaten it all up!"

42

43

Then the three bears saw the chairs by the fireplace.

"Someone's been sitting in my chair!"

said daddy bear in a big booming voice.

"Someone's been sitting in my chair!"

said mommy bear in a middle-sized voice.

"Someone's been sitting in my chair!"

cried baby bear in a squeaky little voice,

"and they've broken it!"

Next, the bears climbed the stairs up to their bedroom.

"Someone's been sleeping in my bed!"

said daddy bear in a **big** booming voice.

"Someone's been sleeping in my bed!"

said mommy bear in a middle-sized voice.

"Someone's been sleeping in my bed!"

cried baby bear in a squeaky little voice,

"and she's still there!"

At that very moment, Goldilocks woke
up and saw the three bears staring at her.

She had never been so frightened!

She leapt out of bed and
ran as fast as her legs could
carry her, out of the door,
through the forest, and far, far
away from the three bears' cottage.

Goldilocks never went there
again, and everyone lived
happily ever after.

True or false?

Now that you have read the story, can you answer these true or false questions correctly?

1. Mommy bear made eggs for breakfast.
True or false?

2. Daddy, mommy, and baby bear's chairs were in the garden.
True or false?

3. Goldilocks broke baby bear's chair.
True or false?

4. Goldilocks was tired.
True or false?

5. Mommy bear's bed was too soft.
True or false?

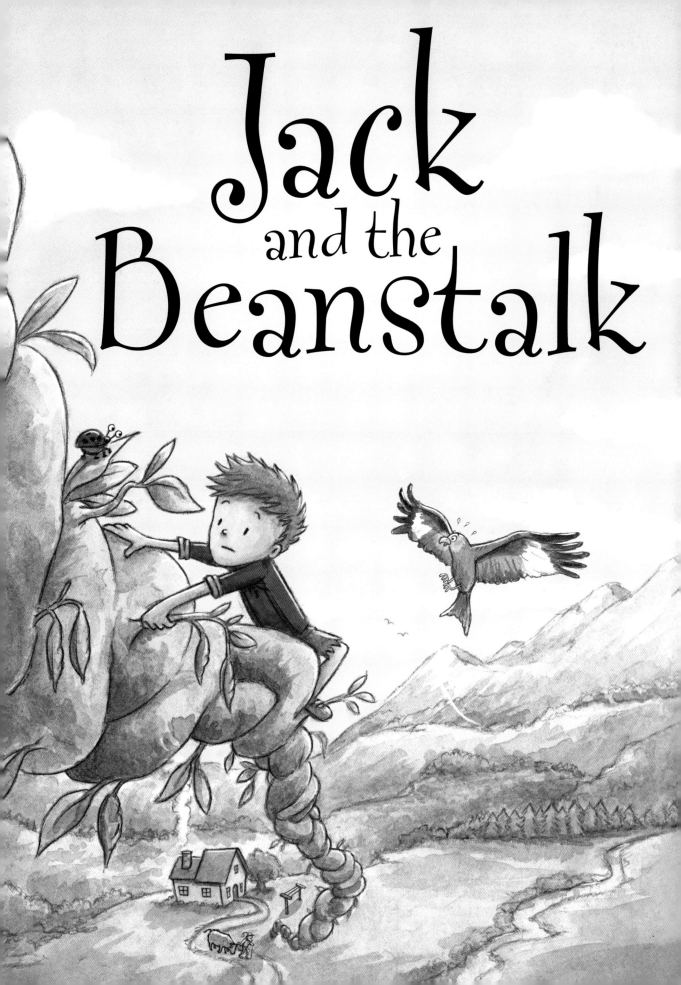

Jack
and the
Beanstalk

Once upon a time there was a boy
called Jack who lived with his mother.

They lived in a little house in the
countryside, where they owned a cow,
but they were very poor.

One day, Jack's mother said,
"Take the cow to market and sell her
for as much money as you can."

Jack had not gone far before he met an old man.

"I'll give you five beans for your cow," said the old man.

"Five beans!" replied Jack.

"Why would I want five beans?"

54

"These are magic beans!" replied the old man.
"They will bring you luck."

Jack was excited at the thought of magic beans, so he gave the cow to the old man and took them.

When Jack got home, his mother was very angry.

"You sold the cow **for five beans!**" she shouted. "Now we have nothing!"

She threw the beans out of the window and sent Jack to bed without any supper.

But the beans really **were** magic, and during the night they started to grow.

The next morning when Jack woke up, there was a **giant** beanstalk outside his window!

57

Before his mother could stop him, Jack climbed up to the top of the beanstalk! There he saw the most magnificent castle.

He went inside to look around. Then he heard a fierce voice.

"Fee, fi, fo, fum,
I smell the blood
of an
Englishman!
Be he alive

or be
he dead,
I'll grind his
bones to make
my bread!"

It was a **terrible ogre!**

Quickly, Jack hid in a cupboard. The ogre
searched the castle, but he could not find Jack.

The ogre gave up looking and
put a hen on the table.

"Lay!" bellowed the ogre,
banging his fist.

The hen laid an egg –
not an ordinary egg but a

golden
egg!

The ogre then ate a huge meal and fell asleep in his chair.

Jack saw his chance. He picked up the hen and ran for the door.

"Help, Master!"
    clucked the hen.

The ogre woke up and ran
after Jack, but quick as a flash,

Jack
slid
down
the
beanstalk.

Jack was so fast the ogre did not see where he went.

Jack's mother was cross, but she could not stay angry for long when she saw the hen lay a golden egg.

A few days later, when his mother was out,
Jack climbed up the beanstalk again!

Jack tiptoed into the ogre's kitchen
and hid in the cupboard once
more. The ogre was sitting
at the table, counting
golden coins.

"Fee, fi, fo, fum,
I smell the blood
of an
Englishman!

Be he alive or be
he dead,

I'll grind his bones

to make my
bread!"

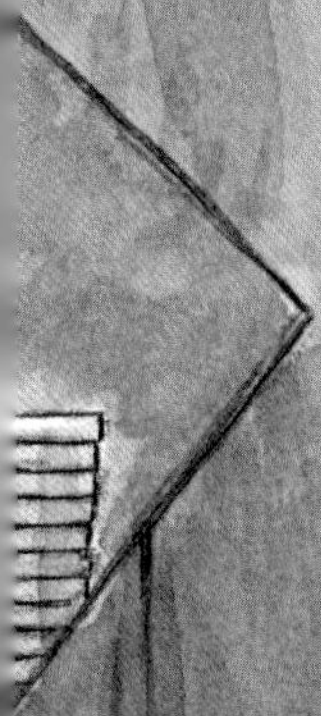

The ogre searched the castle, but again he could not find Jack. He put his magic golden harp on the table.

"Play!" bellowed the ogre, banging his fist.

As the harp began to play, it sent the ogre quickly to sleep.

Jack saw his chance. He picked up the harp and ran for the door.

"Help, Master!"
sang the harp.

The ogre woke up immediately.

He saw Jack running toward the beanstalk and chased after him.

Jack slid down the beanstalk.

But this time the ogre followed.

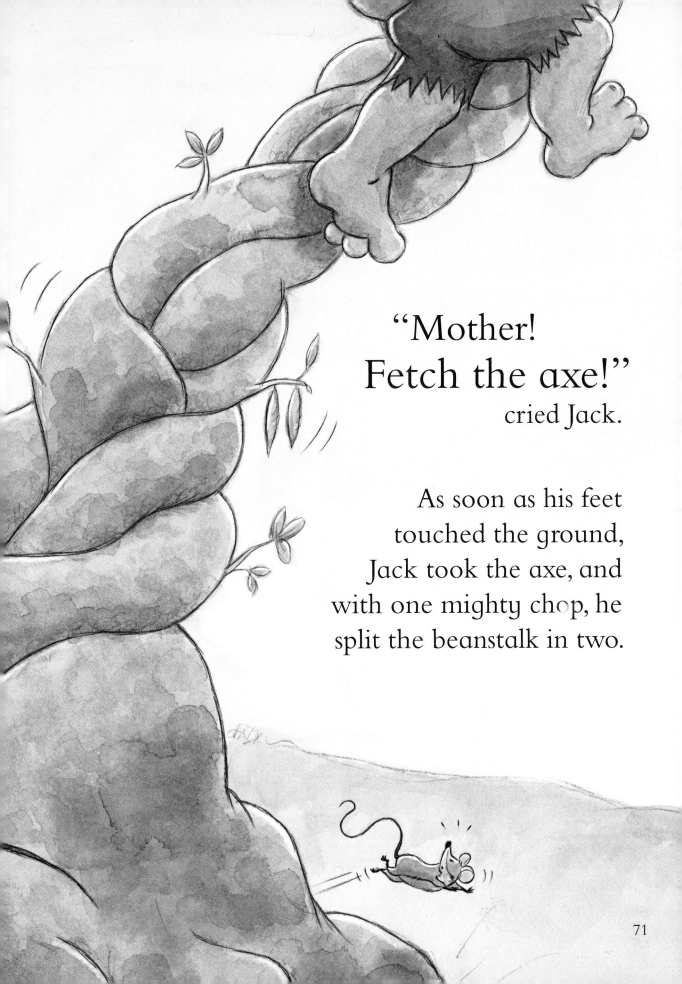

"Mother!
Fetch the axe!"
cried Jack.

As soon as his feet
touched the ground,
Jack took the axe, and
with one mighty chop, he
split the beanstalk in two.

The terrible ogre came crashing down,
and that was the end of him!

Now that Jack and his mother had a
hen that laid golden eggs, and a magic
harp, they were no longer poor.

They lived
happily ever after.

Who's who?

Based on what they are saying, can you guess which character from the story each speech bubble belongs to?

"I said, 'Fee, fi, fo, fum!' Who am I?"

"I was cross with Jack for swapping our cow for beans! Who am I?"

"I laid a golden egg. Who am I?"

"I had a mouse on my hat! Who am I?"

"My music sent the ogre to sleep. What am I?"

"I climbed up the beanstalk. Who am I?"

Cinderella

Once upon a time a girl called
Cinderella lived with her stepmother
and two ugly stepsisters.

Cinderella's stepmother and stepsisters
were cruel. They made her do all the
work around the house while they
did nothing.

'Cinderella' was the name they gave her because she slept among the cinders and ashes by the fire.

Cinderella dressed in rags and clogs, while the ugly stepsisters wore beautiful dresses.

One day, the girls each received an invitation to the handsome prince's ball. Cinderella was thrilled to hear about the ball, but her stepmother said,

"You are NOT allowed to go to the ball, Cinderella!"

"But you will have to help your stepsisters get ready!"

The day of the ball came, and the ugly
stepsisters were getting dressed.

"Fetch me this,
    Cinderella!"

"Fetch me that, Cinderella!"

the ugly stepsisters said.

Cinderella wished
she could go to the
ball with them.
She felt very sad
and started to cry.

After they left, Cinderella continued to cry, but then something magical happened! Cinderella's fairy godmother appeared.

"Don't cry, Cinderella. You shall go to the ball!"

she said.

"Fetch me a pumpkin from the garden, two white mice from the cellar, and a rat from the yard."

Cinderella found them all and placed them on the ground. The fairy godmother waved her magic wand.

In an instant, the pumpkin became a glittering carriage, the mice two magnificent horses, and the rat a finely dressed coachman.

Then, with a touch of her wand, the fairy godmother turned Cinderella's rags into a ball gown fit for a princess! Her wooden clogs became the daintiest of glass slippers, and Cinderella was ready to go to the ball.

"Enjoy the ball, Cinderella. But you must be home before the clock strikes twelve because the spell will be broken at midnight!"

warned the fairy godmother.

When Cinderella arrived at the ball, she looked so beautiful that her ugly stepsisters did not recognize her.

Everyone wondered who this lovely young girl was.

The handsome prince danced every single dance with her, and Cinderella had never been so happy.

But soon it would be twelve o'clock.

As the clock
began to
chime,
Cinderella
remembered
what the fairy godmother
had said, and she ran quickly
from the room.

The handsome prince ran after her, but all he
found was a glass slipper. As she ran into the
distance, Cinderella's ball gown turned back to
rags and her carriage became a pumpkin again!

The white mice
scurried back to the
cellar, and the rat
followed them home
to the yard.

The morning after the ball, the handsome prince was determined to find the girl whose foot the glass slipper fit.

He did not know her name, but he knew he loved her.

He was going to visit every house in the land in search of his princess.

He searched far and wide, without any success, until finally he came to Cinderella's home.

The ugly stepsisters each tried on the glass slipper.

They pushed and pushed their toes into the dainty shoe, but their feet were much too big.

"Do you have another daughter?" the handsome prince asked Cinderella's stepmother.

"You mean Cinderella?"
laughed the ugly stepsisters.

"But she
only wears
wooden clogs!"

Cinderella was called in from the kitchen.

She put the glass slipper on her foot –
and it fit her perfectly!

"At last, I have found my princess!"

said the handsome prince.

The handsome prince whisked Cinderella back to his palace where they lived happily ever after.

And the ugly stepsisters – they were green with envy!

True or false?

Now that you have read the story, can you answer these true or false questions correctly?

1. The ugly stepsisters were cruel to Cinderella.

   True or false?

2. The mice became two pumpkins.

   True or false?

3. The rat became a coachman.

   True or false?

4. The spell was broken at midnight.

   True or false?

5. The slipper fit the ugly stepsisters perfectly.

   True or false?

The Three Little Pigs

Once upon a time there were three little pigs. It was a big day for the little pigs because they were leaving home for the first time.

"Be careful, my little piggy-wigs," said Mother Pig, kissing each little pig on its chinny, chin, chin.

"Don't trust the **big bad wolf**. He will eat you if he gets the chance!"

The three little pigs set off down the road.
Soon they met a boy selling straw.

"I can use this straw to build myself a house,"
said the first little pig.

"Please can I buy some of your straw?"
he asked the boy.

So the first little pig planned to build his house from straw.

"This will be a lovely, comfy house!" said the first little pig.

"I am sure I will be happy here!"

The other little pigs carried on down the road. Soon they met a girl selling wood.

"I can use this wood to build myself a house," said the second little pig.

"Please can I buy some of your wood?" he asked the girl.

So the second little pig started to build his house from wood.

"This will be a warm, cozy house!" said the second little pig.

"I am sure I will be happy here!"

The third little pig carried on down the road.
Soon he met a man selling bricks.

"I can use these bricks to build myself a house,"
said the third little pig.

"Please can I buy some of your bricks?"
he asked the man.

So the third little pig started to build his house from bricks.

"This will be a good, strong house!" said the third little pig.

"I am sure I will be happy here!"

The three little pigs were very happy.
They were so busy finishing their houses that
they did not see the **big bad wolf** spying on
them from the bushes.

The **big bad wolf** licked his lips when he saw the three little pigs.

He wanted to eat them!

The next day the **big bad wolf** went to visit the first little pig. He tapped lightly on the door.

"Little pig, little pig, let me come in!"
said the **big bad wolf**.

"Not by the hair on my chinny, chin, chin! I will not let you in!" said the first little pig.

"Then I'll **huff**, and I'll **puff**, and I'll **blow your house down!**"

said the **big bad wolf**.

So he huffed, and he puffed, and he blew the straw house down!

The little pig ran just in time to his brother's house and escaped from the **big bad wolf!**

The next day the **big bad wolf** went to visit the second little pig. He knocked loudly on the door.

"Little pig, little pig, let me come in!" said the **big bad wolf**.

"Not by the hair on my chinny, chin, chin! I will not let you in!" said the second little pig.

"Then I'll **huff**, and I'll **puff**, and I'll **blow your house down!**" said the **big bad wolf**.

So he huffed, and he puffed, and he blew the wooden house down!

The little pigs ran to their brother's brick house and managed to escape from the **big bad wolf!**

113

The next day the **big bad wolf** went to visit the third little pig. He banged hard on the door.

"Little pig, little pig, let me come in!" said the **big bad wolf**.

"Not by the hair on my chinny, chin, chin! I will not let you in!" said the third little pig.

"Then I'll **huff,** and I'll **puff,** and I'll **blow your house down!"** said the **big bad wolf**.

So he huffed, and he **puffed**, and he **huffed**, and he **puffed** again ... but he could not blow the brick house down!

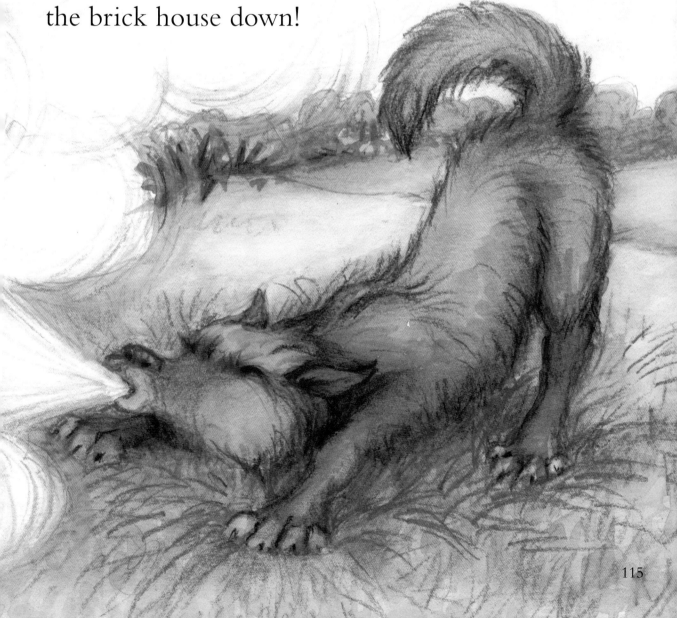

Then the **big bad wolf** had an idea ...

he could

climb down

the chimney!

On to the roof
he jumped,
quick as
a flash!

116

But the third little pig had an idea too ...

He put a large pot of
hot water on the fire!

When the wolf came down the chimney,
he went SPLASH into the water!
It burned his bottom, and he went running
out of the door, never to be seen again.

Then the three little pigs all
lived happily ever after!

True or false?

Now that you have read the story, can you answer these true or false questions correctly?

1. The **big bad wolf** was kind.
   True or false?

2. The **big bad wolf** wanted to eat the pigs.
   True or false?

3. The first pig's house was made out of jelly.
   True or false?

4. The second pig built his house from wood.
   True or false?

5. The strongest house was built from straw.
   True or false?

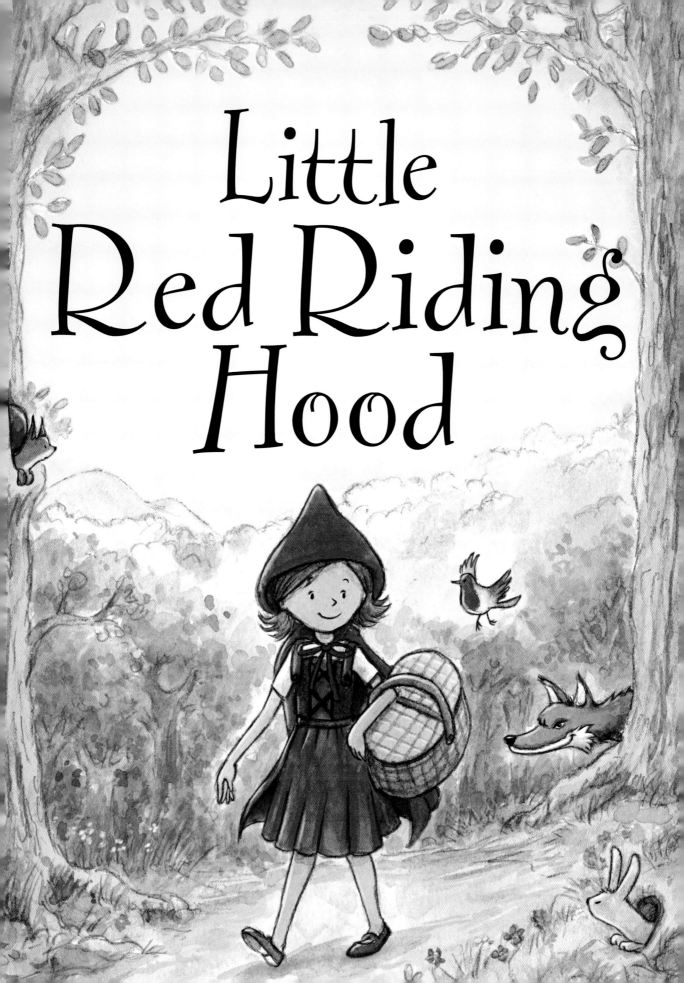

Little Red Riding Hood

Once upon a time there lived a girl called Little Red Riding Hood.

Everyone called her this because she always wore a red cloak and hood.

One day Little Red Riding Hood's mother asked her to take some bread and cakes to her Grandma, who lived in the middle of a forest.

Little Red Riding Hood set off down the path to her Grandma's cottage in the forest. She passed a friendly woodcutter on the way.

A **wicked wolf** was watching her, and as she came closer he stepped out from behind a tree.

"Hello,
Little Red
Riding Hood,"
he said, smiling.

"Where are you
going?"

"To see my
Grandma," she replied.

"Where does your
Grandma live?"
asked the
wicked wolf.

"In the cottage under
the big oak tree,"
she replied.

The **wicked wolf** was very hungry.
He thought Little Red Riding Hood
would taste good to eat!

He wanted to get to Grandma's cottage
before she did, so he quickly said goodbye.

The **wicked wolf** went straight to the cottage under the big oak tree. He knocked on the door, pretending to be Little Red Riding Hood.

"It's me, Grandma!" he said in a squeaky voice.

"Lift the latch and come in, my dear," Grandma replied.

As soon as he stepped inside, the **wicked wolf** pounced on Grandma. He swallowed her in one gulp!

Quickly, he put on a nightdress and cap. Then he jumped into bed and waited.

When Little Red Riding Hood arrived at the cottage, she saw that the door was open.

"It's me, Grandma!" she called out.

There was no reply, so she went upstairs to Grandma's bedroom.

'Grandma'
was in bed,
but she looked
different.

"Grandma,
    what **big ears** you have!"
        said Little Red Riding Hood.

"All the better to **hear** you with, my dear!"
        replied the
        wicked wolf.

"Grandma, what **big eyes** you have!" said Little Red Riding Hood.

"All the better to **see** you with, my dear! Come closer, child!" replied the **wicked wolf**.

"Oh Grandma,
what big **teeth** you have!"
cried Little Red Riding Hood.

"All the
better to
EAT
you with!"
the **wicked wolf**
snarled.

Then he sprang out of bed and swallowed
Little Red Riding Hood in one gulp!

The friendly woodcutter had just finished his work and decided to call in at Grandma's for a cup of tea.

136

When he arrived, the door was open, and Little Red Riding Hood's basket was on the table.

"Grandma!
Little Red Riding Hood!"

he called out.

There was no reply, so he went upstairs to look for them.

The **wicked wolf** was hiding under the bedclothes.

But when the
woodcutter came
into the room, the
wicked wolf
leapt out of bed.

The woodcutter saw the **wicked wolf's** big stomach and knew he must have eaten Grandma and Little Red Riding Hood.

So he lifted his axe, and with one blow, he killed the **wicked wolf!**

Then he cut open the
wicked wolf's stomach and out came
Grandma and Little Red Riding Hood!

They were unhurt because the **wicked wolf**
had swallowed them whole.

Grandma made them all a cup of tea, and they ate the cakes that Little Red Riding Hood had brought.

And they all lived **happily ever after.**

Who's who?

Based on what they are saying, can you guess which character from the story each speech bubble belongs to?

"I'm watching Little Red Riding Hood and her mother in the kitchen. Who am I?"

"There was a picture of me with Grandma on the wall in her house. Who am I?"

"I thought Little Red Riding Hood would taste good to eat! Who am I?"

"The wicked wolf wore my nightdress and cap! Who am I?"

"I saved Grandma and Little Red Riding Hood. Who am I?"

"I sat on the friendly woodcutter's axe when he went into Grandma's house. Who am I?"

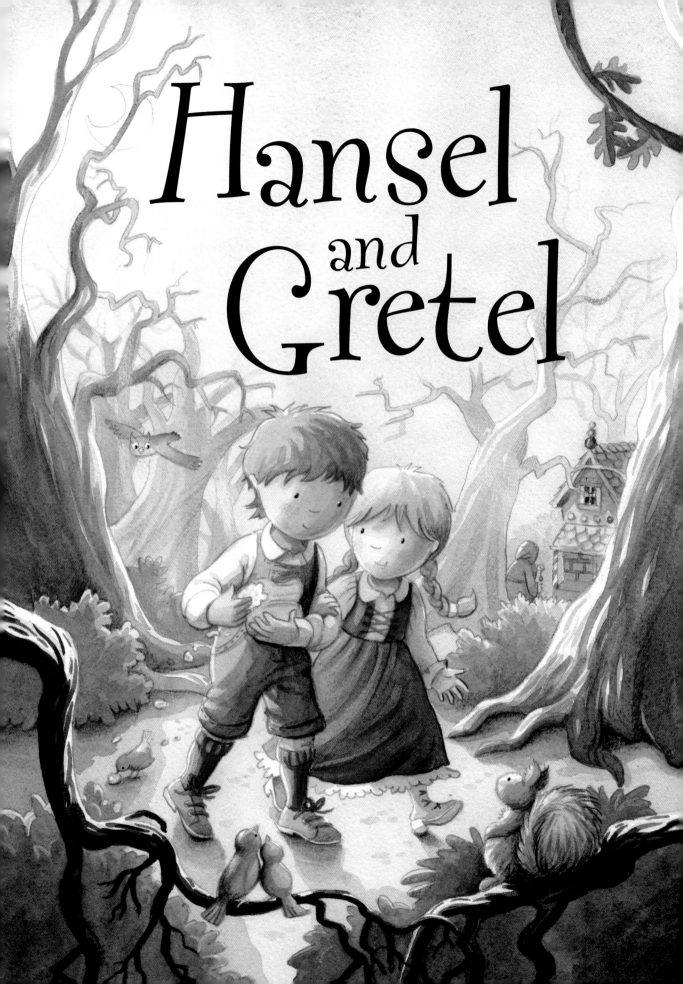

Hansel and Gretel

Once upon a time there was a boy called Hansel
and a girl called Gretel.

They lived with their father, who was a
poor woodcutter, and their cruel stepmother.
Often they went to bed hungry.

One night, they heard
their stepmother say,

"We have only enough food
for ourselves. Tomorrow we will
have to take the children into the
woods and leave them there."

Gretel cried and cried,
but Hansel had a plan.

"Don't worry," he said to Gretel.
"I will look after you."

Once everyone was asleep, Hansel
crept outside and filled his pockets
with white pebbles. Then he went
back to bed.

The next day,
their stepmother and father
took them into the woods.
Hansel stayed back, and as they
walked along, he dropped the
pebbles onto the path.

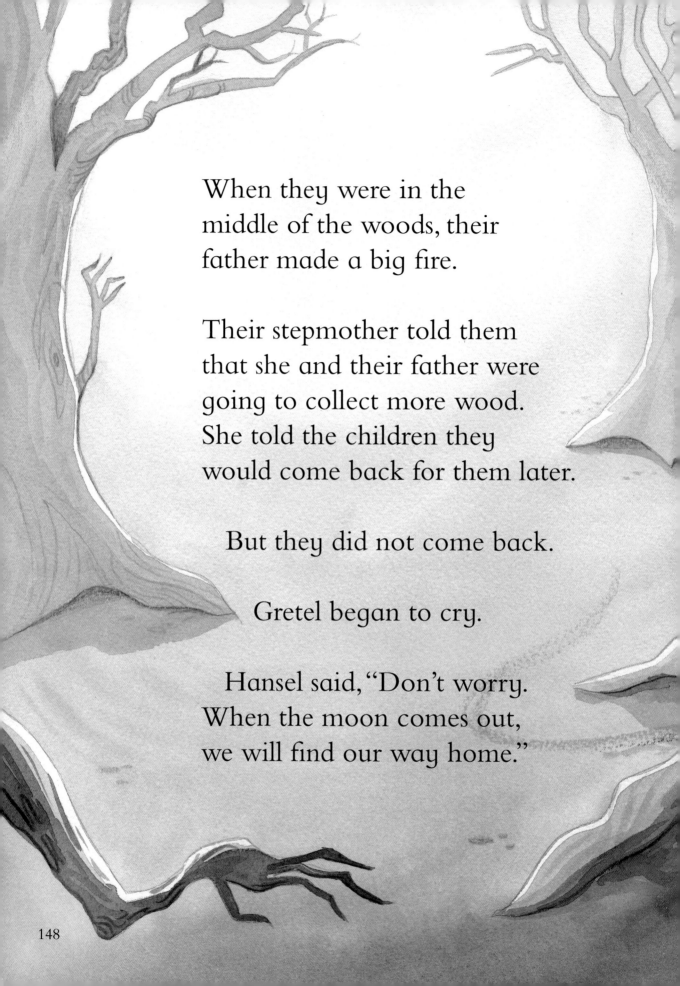

When they were in the
middle of the woods, their
father made a big fire.

Their stepmother told them
that she and their father were
going to collect more wood.
She told the children they
would come back for them later.

But they did not come back.

Gretel began to cry.

Hansel said, "Don't worry.
When the moon comes out,
we will find our way home."

148

At last the moon came out, and the white pebbles shone brightly in the moonlight. Hansel and Gretel followed the trail of pebbles all the way back home!

When their father saw them, he was so pleased.

Their stepmother,
however, was not happy.
That night, they heard her say,

"Tomorrow we will have
to take the children deeper
into the woods and leave
them there."

When everyone was asleep, Hansel crept downstairs to get some more pebbles, but this time the door was locked.

He went back to bed empty-handed and very sad.

The next day, their stepmother woke them up early.

She gave them each a piece of bread.
Then she took them deep into the woods.

As they walked along, Hansel
dropped crumbs of bread onto the
path behind them.

They reached the
deepest part of the
woods, where their
stepmother told them to
wait. She said she would
come back for them later.
Hansel and Gretel waited,
but she did not come back.

Gretel shared her bread
with Hansel, and soon
it grew dark.

Hansel said, "Don't worry. When the moon comes out, we will follow the trail of breadcrumbs home."

At last, the moon came out. But Hansel and Gretel could not see the breadcrumbs.

The hungry birds had eaten them all!

Hansel and Gretel were lost in
the woods and spent the night
huddled together. The next day
when they awoke, they saw a white
bird singing in a tree. It had such a
lovely call that they followed it.
The white bird led them to the
strangest cottage.

They could not believe their eyes!
The cottage was made of gingerbread and
sweets of every kind.

The children were so hungry that they
broke off sweets to eat and failed to
notice the old woman watching them.

The cottage door opened,
and the old woman came out.

She invited them inside and gave them pancakes,
but she was only pretending to be nice.

Really she was a wicked witch!

The **wicked witch** locked Hansel in a cage, and she made Gretel scrub the floor.

Every day the **wicked witch** fed Hansel huge meals. She was fattening him up to cat him!

So Hansel played a trick on her!

When she reached in the cage to feel how fat he was, he stuck out a chicken bone.

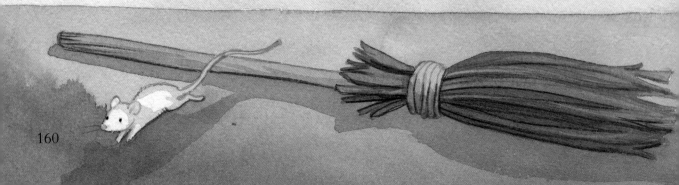

The wicked witch had bad eyesight – so she thought it was his finger. She was disappointed that he was not getting any fatter.

recipes
for
children

One day, the **wicked witch** decided to eat
Hansel anyway – even if he was too thin.
She told Gretel to get into the oven to
check that it was hot enough. She was
really planning to eat Gretel as well!

Clever Gretel pretended she did not know how.
So the **wicked witch** said she would show her.
Gretel saw her chance. She shoved the
wicked witch inside the oven and
quickly locked the door.

Then she freed Hansel from the cage.

Hansel and Gretel found some precious pearls in the **wicked witch**'s cottage.

"These are better than pebbles!" said Hansel. "We can take them back for father." So he put some pearls in his pocket.

They left the cottage, and at last they found the path home.

Their father was overjoyed to see them again and told them that their stepmother had died while they were gone.

Hansel gave him the pearls from the **wicked witch's** cottage. They were able to buy lots of food with the pearls, and they all lived happily ever after.

True or false?

Now that you have read the story, can you answer these true or false questions correctly?

1. Hansel and Gretel's father was a wizard.

   ## True or false?

2. The wicked witch's cottage was made of gold.

   ## True or false?

3. At the end of the story, Hansel and Gretel found their way home.

   ## True or false?

4. Hansel and Gretel bought a horse with the pearls they found in the cottage.

   ## True or false?

5. Hansel left a trail of sweets to find the way home.

   ## True or false?

The Gingerbread Man

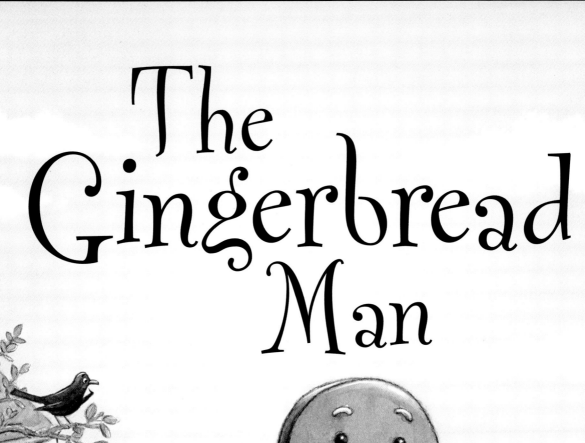

Once upon a time there lived a little
old woman and a little old man.

One day the little old woman made
a gingerbread man.

She made his eyes from two currants,
his mouth from sweet white icing,
and his buttons from red cherries.

Then she put him
on a tray to bake
in the oven.

After a few minutes, she heard a voice coming from inside the oven, shouting,

"Help! Help!"

When the little old woman opened the door, the gingerbread man jumped out.

He ran to the kitchen door as fast as his little gingerbread legs could carry him.

"Come back!" cried the little old man.

The gingerbread man turned his head and laughed.

"Run, run as fast as you can! You can't catch me – I'm the gingerbread man!"

The little old woman and the little old man chased after him. But the gingerbread man was really fast!

He could run faster than the little old woman and faster than the little old man.

Soon the gingerbread man reached
the end of the garden path and carried
on down the lane.

A cow from the farm saw him run past.

"You smell good enough to eat!
Come back!" cried the cow.

The gingerbread man turned his head
and laughed.

"Run, run as fast as you can!
You can't catch me –
I'm the gingerbread man!"

The cow chased after him. But the gingerbread man was really fast!

He could run faster than the cow, faster than the little old woman, and faster than the little old man.

175

Soon the gingerbread man reached the end of the lane, but he carried on running into the fields.

A horse standing there saw him run past.

"You smell good enough to eat! Come back!" cried the horse.

The gingerbread man turned his head
and laughed.

"Run, run as fast as you can!
You can't catch me –
I'm the gingerbread man!"

The horse chased after him. But the gingerbread man was really fast!

He could run faster than the horse, faster than the cow, faster than the little old woman, and faster than the little old man.

The gingerbread man was
enjoying himself.

No one could run fast enough
to catch him!

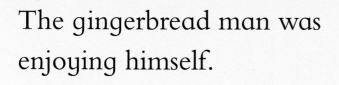

He was running so fast he did not see
the sly fox watching from behind a tree.

Then the gingerbread
man came to a river.

But the gingerbread man had a problem
– he could not swim!

The sly fox said he could help.

"I can take you across the river.
Climb up onto my tail."

The horse, the cow, the little old woman, and the little old man soon reached the riverbank.

Quickly, the gingerbread man climbed up onto the fox's tail, and the fox started to swim.

The sly fox turned his head and said,

"Climb up onto my back so you don't get wet!"

The gingerbread man climbed up onto the fox's back.

As the river got deeper, the sly fox
turned his head again and said,

"Climb up onto my nose
so you don't get wet!"

The gingerbread man climbed
up onto the fox's nose.

Quick as a flash, the sly fox lifted his head and threw the gingerbread man up into the air.

He opened his mouth wide and caught the gingerbread man between his teeth.

Then with one bite, the clever fox
gobbled him up!

And that
was the

end of the
gingerbread man!

Who's who?

Based on what they are saying, can you guess which character from the story each speech bubble belongs to?

"I offered to help the gingerbread man get across the river. Who am I?"

"I started chasing the gingerbread man in the fields. Who am I?"

"I said 'Run, run as fast as you can!' Who am I?"

"I wore oven gloves. Who am I?"

"I am black and white. Who am I?"

"I was the first one to shout 'Come back!' Who am I?"